PARTS OF A PLANT

A Look at Leaves

Lindsey Lowe

KidHaven
PUBLISHING

Published in 2020 by
KidHaven Publishing, an Imprint of
Greenhaven Publishing, LLC
353 3rd Avenue
Suite 255
New York, NY 10010

For Brown Bear Books Ltd:
Text and Editor: Lindsey Lowe
Children's Publisher: Anne O'Daly
Design Manager: Keith Davis
Picture Manager: Sophie Mortimer

Picture Credits
t=top, c=center, b=bottom, l=left, r=right
Interior: Alamy: Friedrich Stark 18; iStock: cobraphoto 21, hadynyah 16, joakimbkk 4, JulieJJ
13t, Lezh 14, Sasin Paraksa 11b, Simplyphotos 12; Shutterstock: 13Smile 20, Meng Chatchai
5b, dihca 11t, Lukas Gojda 10, Anya Ivanova 19b, Matt Jeppson 15t, Kingarion 15b, lewalp
17b, R Moore 9b, Myimages – Micha 13b, Ohishiapply 19t, Rafal Olkis 7,Valentina Razumova
6, Julia Sudnitskaya 10r, Ajay Tvm 5t, 8, Tomfey Zadvornov 9t.

All other photos and artwork, Brown Bear Books.

Brown Bear Books has made every attempt to contact the copyright holder.
If anyone has any information about omissions please contact licensing@brownbearbooks.co.uk

Cataloging-in-Publication Data

Names: Lowe, Lindsey.
Title: A look at leaves / Lindsey Lowe.
Description: New York : KidHaven Publishing, 2020. | Series: Parts of a plant | Includes glossary
and index.
Identifiers: ISBN 9781534533691 (pbk.) | ISBN 9781534533714 (library bound) | ISBN
9781534533707 (6 pack) | ISBN 9781534533721 (ebook)
Subjects: LCSH: Leaves--Juvenile literature. | Leaves--Physiology--Juvenile literature. | Plant
anatomy--Juvenile literature.
Classification: LCC QK649.L694 2020 | DDC 581.4'8--dc23

Manufactured in the United States of America

CPSIA Compliance Information: Batch-#BW20KL:
For further information contact Greenhaven Publishing LLC, New York, New York at 1-844-317-7404.

Contents

What Are Leaves?

Leaves are a plant's solar panels. **They absorb sunlight to make food for the plant.**

Most leaves are green. Some plants have just a few leaves. But most plants have many leaves. Together, a plant's leaves are called its foliage.

Leaf Parts

The broad part of a leaf is called the blade. Small veins run across the blade. Veins carry water and sugars to and from the leaf. The big vein along the middle of the leaf is called the midrib. A leaf with one blade attached to a stem is a simple leaf. A leaf with two or more blades attached to a stem is a compound leaf.

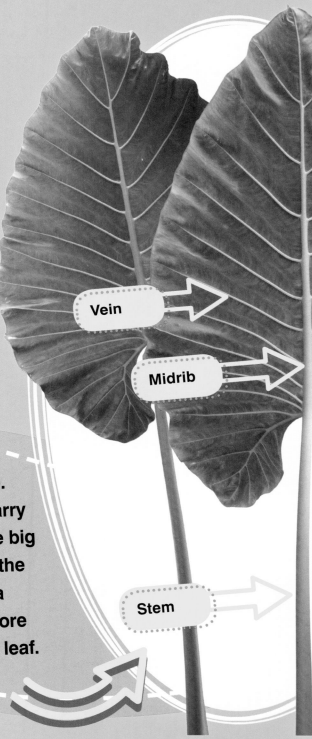

Vein

Midrib

Stem

Leaf Shapes

Leaves come in all shapes and sizes. Some are oval. Some are heart-shaped or triangular. Some, like these mimosa leaves, have lots of little leaves, or "leaflets."

THAT'S AMAZING!

The giant water lily has huge leaves. They can grow up to 6 feet (1.8 m) across. They float on the surface of the water. The leaves are very strong. They can hold weights of up to 136 pounds (62 kg). Animals, and even people, can stand on the leaves without sinking!

What Do Leaves Do?

Plants make their own food. The leaves use sunlight, carbon dioxide, and water to make sugar.

Leaves contain a green chemical called chlorophyll. Chlorophyll helps plants make food. This process is called photosynthesis. Photosynthesis also produces oxygen. The leaves release oxygen into the air. Animals and plants need oxygen to breathe.

Leaves use energy from sunshine to make sugars from air and water.

Sun

1

2

3

Photosynthesis

1. The leaves take in sunlight.

2. Carbon dioxide from the air enters the leaf through tiny holes.

3. Roots, stems, and veins carry water from the soil to the leaves.

4. Energy from the sun lets the water and the carbon dioxide combine. It makes a type of sugar in the leaves to feed the plant.

5. The leaves release oxygen into the air.

THAT'S AMAZING!

Carbon dioxide is a gas. It is not always produced naturally. When people burn fossil fuels, too much carbon dioxide is released into the air. This leads to the greenhouse effect and heats up our planet. Plants can help. They take carbon dioxide from the air and breathe it out as oxygen!

Why Leaves Change

Most leaves change with the seasons. New leaves appear in spring. They live until the winter.

All leaves begin as buds. Buds have a tough covering. It protects them from cold in the winter. The buds open in the spring. The leaves make food for the plant through the summer.

A New Leaf

1. When the bud first opens, the new leaf is small and curly. 2. The leaf begins to flatten out. It grows in the warm sunshine. 4. Soon it grows into a full-size leaf. It is ready to make food for the plant from the summer sunshine.

THAT'S AMAZING!

Chlorophyll makes leaves green. But leaves are naturally orange and yellow! The green covers up the other colors. When leaves stop making food in fall, they lose the chlorophyll. The other colors show through. That is why leaves turn red and gold in fall.

Winter

In summer, there is lots of sun and water for leaves to make food. In winter, the sun shines less. Water is often frozen. Cold weather kills the leaves. They turn brown and their stalks weaken. The dead leaves fall to the ground.

Evergreen Leaves

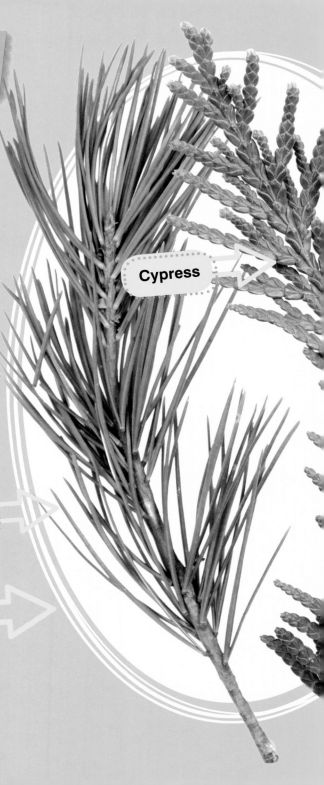

Not all plants drop their leaves in winter. Plants with leaves all year round are called evergreens.

Evergreens grow all over the world. They have green or greenish-blue leaves. Pine trees, cypress trees, holly, and redwood trees are all evergreens. They can survive freezing winters. Evergreens also grow in tropical rain forests. Most tropical plants are evergreens.

Cypress

Pine

Pine trees have evergreen leaves shaped like needles. Cypresses have evergreen leaves with tiny, soft scales.

THAT'S AMAZING!

Most pine leaves or needles are less than 4 inches (10 cm) long. The coulter pine has needles more than 1 foot (0.3 m) long. It also has huge seed cones. Each cone weighs up to 11 pounds (5 kg). That's as heavy as a pet cat!

Pine Needles

Pine trees grow in places with cold, dry winters and hot, dry summers. Pine needles have a waxy coating. The coating helps the leaf store water. It also protects it from pollution.

Leaves and Animals

Leaves don't just make food for plants. They also provide meals for all kinds of animals.

Animals from huge elephants to tiny insects eat leaves. Those that eat leaves directly from trees and bushes are called browsers. Others that eat leaves from the ground are called grazers. Sheep and cows are grazers. They eat leaves of grass.

Browsers

Antelopes and deer are browsers. So are giraffes and elephants. Giraffes live in Africa. Their long necks help them to pluck leaves from the highest branches.

Nursery Food

Some female insects lay their eggs on leaves. When the young insects hatch, they eat the leaves. This is the caterpillar of the zebra longwing butterfly. It can eat 200 leaves in 10 days!

THAT'S AMAZING!

Leaf-cutter ants cut leaves from trees. They carry the leaves back to their nests. The ants do not eat the leaves. They chew them up and spit them out. Fungus grows on the rotting leaf pulp. Then the ants eat the fungus!

How Leaves Survive

Many animals eat plants. Some have ways to protect their leaves from hungry animals.

Some plants have leaves that are tough to chew. Other leaves have sharp edges. Holly leaves have spikes. Mimosa leaves fold up when they are touched. Many leaves taste bad. Others give a nasty sting.

Thistles

Thistles have very sharp leaves. They put off most predators. But goats have tough mouths. They chew their way through thistles—spikes and all!

THAT'S AMAZING!

Before they turn into butterflies or moths, caterpillars eat hundreds of leaves. Some plants have a way to protect themselves from caterpillars. The leaves give off chemicals that attract wasps. Wasps swarm to the plant and kill the caterpillars!

Using Poisons

Some leaves fight off predators using poison. Mustard leaves, cabbage leaves, and radish leaves taste nice to people. But the leaves contain chemicals that can kill small insects if they eat them.

Leaves that People Eat

Leaves are packed with vitamins and minerals. Many leaves taste good and keep us healthy.

Many vegetables have big, soft, green leaves. They include cabbages, spinach, chard, kale, lettuce, and sprouts. Dark green leafy vegetables contain vitamin C, vitamin K, iron, and calcium.

Leaves for Flavor

Herbs help to make food taste better. Here are some popular herbs. You can buy them fresh or dried in supermarkets. How many have you tried?

Parsley

Thyme

THAT'S AMAZING!

Tea is made from the leaves of the tea plant. China grows the most tea. It produces millions of pounds every year. About 2.16 billion cups of tea are drunk around the world every day!

A woman picks tea in India. India is the second-largest producer of tea in the world.

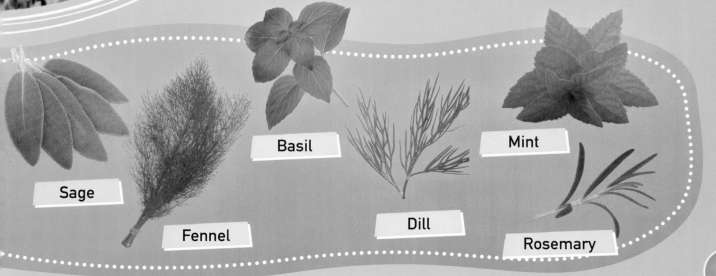

Sage

Fennel

Basil

Dill

Mint

Rosemary

Other Uses for Leaves

People don't just eat leaves. They use leaves to make medicine and fabric. Leaves also provide shelter.

Palm leaves are large and strong. They have many uses. They can be used to make roofs and fences. Strips can be woven to make baskets and hats. Pineapple leaves are used to make a fabric that looks like cotton.

Banana Leaves

Banana leaves can grow up to 6 feet (2 m) long. In the tropics, where bananas grow, people use banana leaves as umbrellas. They also use them as plates. In some countries, the leaves are used in place of plastic bags in supermarkets.

Fabric Dyes

Leaves can be used to make natural dyes. The leaves are dried and ground into powder. Indigo leaves make blue dye. Henna leaves make brownish-red dye. Other leaves will give other colors.

THAT'S AMAZING!

Before modern-day medicine, plants were used to treat people when they were sick. Herbal medicines are still used today. The fleshy leaves of aloe vera contain a chemical that helps to stop the growth of bacteria. It is used to soothe skin problems.

Grow It!

Lettuces are quick and easy to grow from seeds. Plants will keep growing new leaves from spring to fall. Ask an adult to buy the seeds and some multipurpose compost.

Here's How

✿ Use a container that is more than 6 inches (15 cm) deep. Almost any container will do. Use the bottom of a plastic water bottle if you don't have a plant pot. The container should have holes in the bottom for water to drain away.

✿ Fill the container with compost until it is about 1 inch (2.5 cm) below the rim. Smooth the surface.

✿ Push the seeds into the compost 0.5 inch (1.2 cm) apart. Cover with a thin layer of compost. Spray the compost with water. When the plants begin to grow, water the compost regularly. After six to eight weeks, the lettuce leaves will be ready to eat.

✿ Cut off individual leaves using scissors. Leave 1 inch (2.5 cm) of the plant in the pot. It will regrow leaves once or twice more before it is finished.

Cook It!

Caesar salad is a delicious way to enjoy lettuce!

¼ cup grated Parmesan cheese
¼ cup mayonnaise
2 tablespoons milk
1 tablespoon lemon juice
1 garlic clove, peeled
      and chopped

pinch of black pepper
romaine lettuce leaves
toasted croutons
grated Parmesan to sprinkle

WARNING
Be careful when you are chopping ingredients. Make sure an adult kitchen assistant is around to help!

Here's How

1 Put the Parmesan cheese, mayonnaise, milk, lemon juice, garlic, and black pepper in a mixing bowl.

2 Whisk the ingredients together until they are well combined and smooth.

3 Wash and shred the romaine lettuce leaves. Put them in a large bowl. Pour the dressing over the lettuce leaves and toss gently to coat evenly.

4 Add the croutons and sprinkle with grated Parmesan cheese. Serve immediately.

Glossary

blade The flat surface of a leaf.

browser A leaf-eating animal.

bud A curled-up new leaf.

chlorophyll A green chemical in leaves. It helps the leaf use sunlight to make sugary plant food.

evergreen A plant that keeps its leaves green all year round.

foliage All the leaves on a plant.

fossil fuels Natural fuels formed millions of years ago from the remains of animals and plants.

grazer A grass-eating animal.

greenhouse effect The warming of Earth's surface and the air above it caused by gases in the air that trap the energy from the sun.

midrib The stiff vein down the center of a leaf.

nutrients Substances necessary for a plant or animal to grow.

oxygen A gas in the air. It makes water when combined with hydrogen.

photosynthesis The way leaves use energy from sunlight to make sugary food for a plant.

predator An animal that gets its food from other animals or organisms.

Further Resources

Books

DK, Smithsonian. *Trees, Leaves, Flowers, and Seeds* (Smithsonian). New York: DK Children, 2019.

Schuh, Mari C. *I See Fall Leaves.* Minneapolis, MN: Lerner Publications, 2017**.**

Owen, Ruth. *What Do Roots, Stems, Leaves, and Flowers Do?* (World of Plants). New York: PowerKids Press, 2014.

Waldron, Melanie. *Leaves.* Chicago, IL: Heinemann Library, 2014.

Websites

https://kids.kiddle.co/Leaf

https://www.scienceforkidsclub.com/leaves-change-color.html

Index